Taking Your Camera to
ISRAEL

Ted Park

Steadwell Books

Raintree Steck-Vaughn Publishers

A Harcourt Company

Austin · New York
www.steck-vaughn.com

Published by Raintree Steck-Vaughn Publishers,
an imprint of Steck-Vaughn Company

Library of Congress Cataloging-in-Publication Data
Park, Ted
    Israel / by Ted Park.
        p. cm. — (Taking your camera to)
    Summary: Introduces the geography, points of interest, way of life,
economy, culture, and people of Israel.
    ISBN 0-7398-1801-5
    1. Israel—Juvenile literature. 2. Israel—Pictorial works—Juvenile literature.
[1. Israel.] I. Title. II. Series.

DS118 .P25 2000
956.94—dc21   99-058639

Printed in the United States of America
10 9 8 7 6 5 4 3 2 1 W 03 02 01 00

Photo acknowledgments

Cover, pp.1, 3b, 3d, 4 ©PhotoDisc; p.3a ©Chris Salvo/FPG International; p.3c ©Hanan Isachar/CORBIS; p.5 ©Richard T. Nowitz/CORBIS; p.8 ©Nik Wheeler/CORBIS; p.9 ©PhotoDisc; p.11 ©Telegraph Colour Library/FPG International; p.12 ©Charles & Josette Lenars/CORBIS; pp.13, 15 ©PhotoDisc; p.17 ©Paul A. Souders/CORBIS; p.19a ©Chris Salvo/FPG International; p.19b ©Barry Rosenthal/FPG International; p.20 ©David Rubinger/CORBIS; p.21 ©Dave G. Houser/CORBIS; p.23a ©Scott Markewitz/FPG International; p.23b ©Mark Adams/FPG International; p.25 ©Hanan Isachar/CORBIS; p.27 ©PhotoDisc; p.28a ©Telegraph Colour Library/FPG International; p.28b ©PhotoDisc; p.29a ©Comstock Klips; p.29b, c ©PhotoDisc.

All statistics in the Quick Facts section come from *The New York Times Almanac* (1999) and *The World Almanac* (1999). 96618

Contents

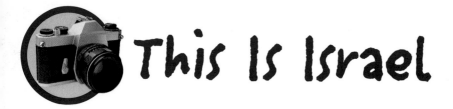

This Is Israel

Israel is a young country. It became a country in 1948. But the land has a very old history. This is where the ancient Jewish people lived. It is where Jesus was born. It is where Mohammed, who started the religion of Islam, was said to rise to heaven. If you took your camera to Israel, you could photograph places that are special to Jewish people, to Christians, and to Muslims.

King Solomon's pillars, a group of sandstone rocks located about 18 miles (30 km) north of the Gulf of Eilat

 4

A view of the port of Haifa

Israel has many interesting cities. One of them is Haifa. Haifa is a seaport in northwest Israel. It is built on the side of a steep hill. Haifa is Israel's chief port.

This book will show you some of the old sights of Israel. It will show you some of the new cities. It will also tell you much about the country. If you know about the country of Israel before you take your camera there, you will enjoy your visit more.

5 📷

The Place

Israel is a small country at the eastern end of the Mediterranean Sea. It is located where Europe meets Africa and Asia. This part of the world is known as the Middle East. Israel is about 300 miles (480 km) long and only about 83 miles (135 km) wide. It is about the size of New Jersey.

Lebanon borders Israel to the north. Syria and Jordan are to the east. On the west is Egypt.

However, Israel has some borders that are not final yet. One of them is the Gaza Strip to the west. Egypt would like this land. Another border that is not final is the West Bank of the Jordan River. This land is in the east. Jordan would like it. A third border that still must be settled is the Golan Heights. This land touches both Syria and Lebanon. It is in the northeast.

The Negev Desert

Although the country is small, it has many different kinds of land. The Negev Desert is in the south. It covers a little more than half of Israel. It is 4,700 square miles (12,172 sq km).

In the east is the Dead Sea. It is a large lake at the southern end of the Jordan River Valley. This is the lowest point on Earth. It is 1,312 feet (400 m) below sea level. The Dead Sea got its name because it is so salty that nothing can live in it. People like to swim there. It is easy for them to float in the salty water.

Lake Kinneret is the lowest freshwater lake in the world. It is 700 feet (212 m) below sea level. This lake is also known as the Sea of Galilee. It is in the northeastern part of Israel.

Most of Israel is dry. Sometimes as many as 5 inches (12.7 cm) of rain fall in 24 hours. When it rains, dry riverbeds fill up. These are called wadis. When they overflow, the water can cause flash floods and mudslides.

The Dead Sea is about nine times as salty as the ocean.

# Jerusalem

Jerusalem is the capital of Israel. It is also one of Israel's oldest cities. Jerusalem is at least 4,000 years old. It was destroyed and rebuilt several times. Jerusalem has three parts.

One part of Jerusalem is the walled Old City. If you took your camera to Jerusalem, this is where you would find many sights to photograph. One famous place in the Old City is the Wailing Wall. This wall is all that remains of an ancient Jewish temple. Jewish people from all over the world come here to pray.

Christians come to the Old City to visit the places where Jesus spent time. Many visit the Church of the Holy Sepulcher. "Sepulcher" is another name for tomb. This church was built on the site where the body of Jesus is thought to have been placed.

Muslims come to the Old City to go to the Dome of the Rock mosque. A mosque is a building where Muslims go to pray. This mosque was built on the place where Mohammed was said to rise to heaven.

 10

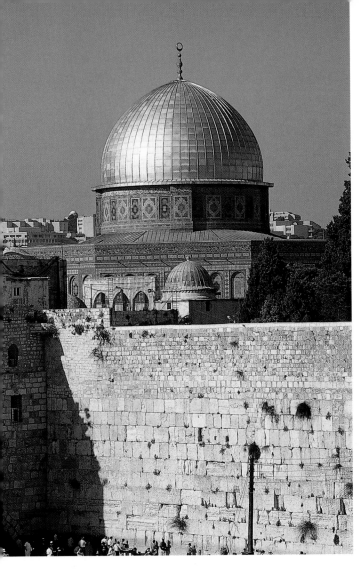

The Wailing Wall (bottom) and the Dome of the Rock mosque (top) are two important places in the Old City.

Another part of the city is East Jerusalem. It is mostly Arab. The third section of Jerusalem is known as West Jerusalem. This is the new part of the city. There are many stores and cafés here.

 # Places to Visit

One of the most popular places to visit in Israel is Masada. It is a fort near the Dead Sea. In A.D. 66 a group of Jewish people tried to fight against the Romans. At that time, Israel was known as Judea. It was part of the Roman Empire. The Jews fought hard but could not win the fight. The Romans controlled the land for many years. They renamed it Palestine.

Masada is a famous place to visit in Israel.

During World War II, about six million Jews died in Europe. Yad Vashem is a memorial to these people. A memorial reminds people of something important. Yad Vashem is near Jerusalem.

After World War II, Jewish people wanted a homeland once again in the land that is now called Israel. On May 14, 1948, Israel became a country. This took place in the city of Tel Aviv. Tel Aviv is on the Mediterranean Sea. It was only built in 1909. Since then the city has become an important center of banking.

The harbor at Tel Aviv

 # The People

There are almost 6 million people living in Israel. People who live in Israel are known as Israelis. Most Israelis are Jewish. In 1950, only a small number of Israel's Jews had been born there. Now that number is larger. Many came from different places, especially after World War II. Some came from Germany and Poland. More recently, Jewish people have come from Ethiopia and from the former Soviet Union. Israel welcomes all Jews who want to become Israeli citizens.

More than one million citizens are not Jewish. Many Arabs live in Israel. About 800,000 of them are Muslim Arabs. About 170,000 are Christian Arabs. Most Christian Arabs live in the large cities.

There are also Bedouins in Israel. Many of these people are nomads. Most Bedouins wander and have no homes. However, some Bedouins do have homes.

Israel has three official languages—Hebrew, Arabic, and English. Many people speak Russian and German. Some also speak Yiddish, a kind of German.

Jews pray at the Wailing Wall in Jerusalem.

15 📷

 Life in Israel

Most Israelis live in cities. Many of them live in small apartments. Some people who live outside the cities may have bigger homes. Many homes are now heated by energy from the sun. This is known as solar energy. Solar heating has become popular in many places.

Israelis who were born in Israel are called sabras. "Sabra" is a Hebrew word that means "prickly pear." This pear is tough on the outside but soft inside. This is the way many Israelis think of themselves. Ever since Israel became a country, Israelis have had to be tough. Building a new country is hard work.

Some people live on a kibbutz. A kibbutz is a farm that is run by the people who live there. They share the work. They also live together and raise their children together.

Many Muslim Arabs live in Israel. They are very friendly and welcome visitors into their homes. In fact, Arabs who give their guests food and drink are well thought of by others.

 16

Jewish men and women between the ages of 18 and 21 have to serve in the army. Men must serve for three years. Women must serve for two years. Older people must serve several weeks each year. Christians and Muslims do not have to serve in the army.

Today, Jews and Arabs live side by side in Israel. But they do not always live in peace.

Melons are grown on a kibbutz.

 Government and Religion

Israel is a parliamentary democracy. This means that members of Israel's parliament are elected. The parliament is called the Knesset. It is made up of 120 people who are elected every four years. The president is chosen by the Knesset for five years. The government of Israel is for all of Israel's people.

Israel promises religious freedom to everyone. Its sites are sacred to Jews, Christians, and Muslims. The Jewish religion is known as Judaism. Many Jews belong to it. But there are large numbers of nonreligious Jews as well. They are known as secular Jews. Most of the Arabs who live in Israel are Muslim, but some are Christian. There are a few Christians who are not Arabs.

**A Muslim in a mosque (above);
a Jew in a synagogue (below)**

19 📷

Earning a Living

Many people who live in Israel work on farms. Because there is not much water in Israel, farmers use irrigation to water the crops. Farmers direct water to the places where it is needed the most. Citrus fruits, melons, and grapes are important crops.

Many Israelis also work in the tourist industry. This is one of Israel's biggest industries. Many Jews, Christians, and Muslims from around the world visit Israel. This is because the country has so much history and meaning for all three religious groups.

Farmers in Israel grow fruits, vegetables, and flowers.

Guides show monuments to the many visitors who come to Israel.

Israel has few natural resources. Natural resources come from nature and are useful to people. The country has only a little oil. Most must be brought in from Egypt. Israel does have some mineral salts and chemicals.

 School and Sports

In Israel children must go to school from ages five to 16. Some schools are run by the state. There are Jewish religious schools, known as yeshivas. There are also Arab schools. Israel has many colleges. People go to these colleges to become teachers, doctors, and lawyers.

Soccer and basketball are the most popular team sports in Israel. The Maccabeah Games are held every four years. They are known as the Jewish Olympics. Israeli athletes compete with others from around the world.

Swimming is popular because the climate of Israel is so hot and sunny. Israelis also enjoy hiking, bicycling, and camping. Skiing is popular on the snowy slopes of Mount Hermon. It is on the border between Israel and Lebanon.

Skiing and swimming are
both popular sports in
Israel.

23

Food and Holidays

Israelis eat a great variety of foods. These include citrus fruits, lamb, rice, and fresh vegetables. All kinds of dishes are popular. This cooking was brought to Israel by people who came there from these parts of the world.

Some Jewish people observe kosher laws. These laws do not allow them to eat pork, game, shellfish, and certain other foods. They also cannot eat meat and dairy products together.

Falafel is a popular Arab food. It is a paste made of chickpeas mashed with oil and then eaten on bread.

Because Israel is important to three different religions, there are three sets of holidays in the country. The Jewish day of worship is the Sabbath. This begins at sundown on Friday and lasts until sundown on Saturday. During this time, families spend time together. Some Jewish holidays include Passover, Rosh Hashanah, and Yom Kippur.

A table set for a meal during a Passover celebration

Christians from all over the world like to celebrate Christmas and Easter in Israel. They often walk along the Via Dolorosa, or the Way of Sorrows. Jesus is thought to have walked to the Crucifixion on this path.

During the month that Muslims call Ramadan, Muslims do not eat or drink during the daytime. At the end of this month, they have a holiday that lasts for three days. It is called Id-ul-fitr.

The Future

If you took your camera to Israel, you would see a young country that is still growing. Many trees are being planted throughout the country. This is helping to make the soil of Israel much better. And through irrigation, farmers are able to grow crops in the desert. Israel grows so many fruits and vegetables that it exports, or sends, many to other countries. This brings money into the country. Israel also exports chemicals, among other things.

However, Israel has some problems. Its main problem is trying to find peace. There has always been a struggle between Jews and Muslims. Most Muslim Arabs still feel that their country was taken away from them when Israel was formed. They would like to get it back.

People all over the world are trying to find ways to help end this problem. So are the Israelis.

Oranges like these grow in Israel because irrigation has provided water for the plants.

When you arrive in Israel, people may greet you by saying "Shalom." And when you leave Israel, they may say the same thing. This is because the word means both "Hello" and "Good-bye." And it also means "Peace."

Quick Facts About
ISRAEL

Capital ▶
Jerusalem

Borders
Lebanon, Syria, Jordan, Egypt

Area
8,019 square miles (20,770 sq km)

Population
5,643,966

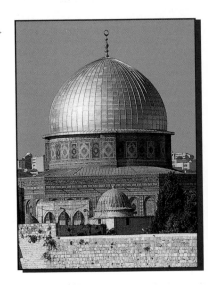

Largest cities
Jerusalem (567,100 people); Tel Aviv-Jaffa (357,400 people); Haifa (246,500 people)

◀ **Chief crops**
citrus and other fruits, vegetables, cotton, beef, poultry, dairy products

Natural resources
copper, phosphates, bromide, potash, clay

Flag of Israel

◀ **Coastline**
170 miles (273 km)

Monetary unit
new Israeli shekel

Literacy rate
95 percent of Israelis can read
and write

Major industries
food processing, diamond cutting
and polishing, textiles, clothing

Glossary

Church of the Holy Sepulcher (SEP-uhl-kuhr) A church in Jerusalem built on the site where the body of Jesus was thought to have been placed

falafel (fuh-LAHF-uhl) A popular Arab food that is made of mashed chickpeas and oil

Haifa (HEYE-fuh) A seaport in northwest Israel

Id-ul-fitr (ID-ul-fitter) A Muslim holiday

irrigation (ear-ah-GAY-shun) A way of watering plants where a farmer directs water to where it is needed

Islam (is-LAHM) The religion begun by Mohammed

Israelis (iz-RAY-leez) People who live in Israel

Judaism (JOOD-ah-iz-uhm) The Jewish religion

Judea (joo-DEE-ah) The name by which Israel was known at the time of Christ

kibbutz (kib-OOTS) A farm that is run by the people who live there

Knesset (kuh-NEHS-et) Israel's governing body

kosher laws (KO-shur) Laws that some Jewish people obey about the types of foods they cannot eat

Masada (muh-SAW-duh) An ancient fort near the Dead Sea

mosque (MAHSK) The building where Muslims pray

Muslim (MUHZ-luhm) A person who follows the teachings of Mohammed

Palestine (PAL-uh-steyen) The name the ancient Romans gave to Israel

parliamentary democracy (par-luh-MENT-uh-ree) A type of government in which members of the country's governing body are elected by the people

Ramadan (RAHM-uh-dahn) The month during which Muslims cannot eat or drink all day long

sabra (SAHB-ruh) A person who was born in Israel

secular Jews (SEK-yuh-luhr) Jewish people who are not religious

Tel Aviv (tell ah-VEEV) A city on the Mediterranean Sea that is an important center of banking

Via Dolorosa (VEE-uh DOH-luh-ROW-suh) The path on which Jesus was taken to the Crucifixion. These words mean "Way of Sorrows."

wadis (WAHD-ees) Riverbeds that have filled with rain

yeshivas (yuh-SHEE-vuhs) Jewish religious schools

Yiddish (YID-ish) A language that is a kind of German

Index